BRUCE MOOSE
and the What-Ifs
◆ ◆ ◆
Gary J. Oliver
with H. Norman Wright
Illustrated by Sharon Dahl

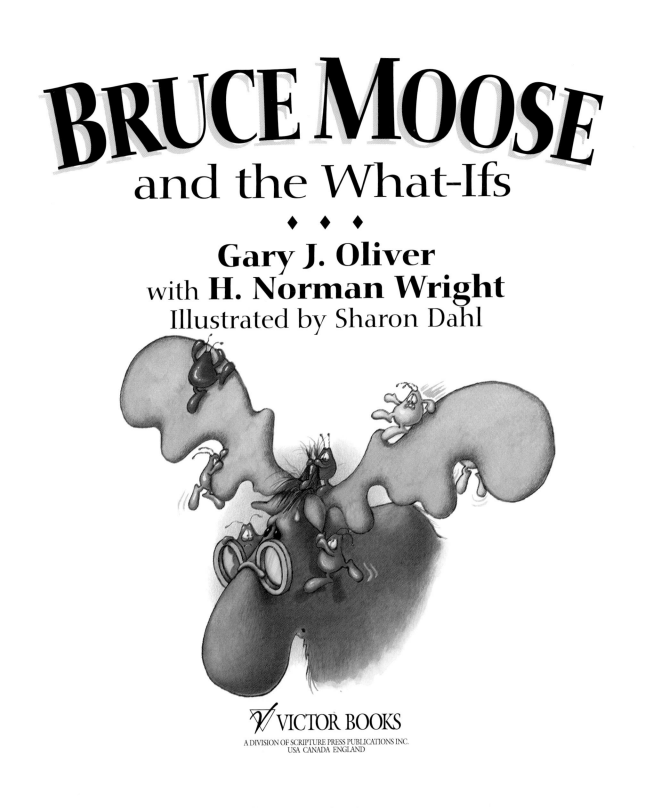

𝒱 VICTOR BOOKS

A DIVISION OF SCRIPTURE PRESS PUBLICATIONS INC.
USA CANADA ENGLAND

Saturday was a special day in Wonder Woods. Every Saturday the young animals from the edge of the forest would follow the path to the big meadow in the center of the woods.

They hopped and skipped and skittered along the path, sliding down the grassy banks, crossing over the bridge, and running into the meadow with great excitement. All along the path the friends would gather, laughing and singing their Saturday song:

"It's Saturday! What do you say?

Let's go to the meadow and play all day!"

One sunny Saturday, Buford Bear crawled out of his den and lumbered down the path. When he passed the oak tree, Ric and Rac scampered out to join him. Soon HipHop Bunny appeared, along with Elwood Elk—who brought Norman Nightcrawler along for the ride. At the gnarly, old, elm tree Brenda Blue Jay joined in. Then, out of nowhere, Shirl Squirrel zipped past, racing circles around all her friends.

But when the happy group at last came to the point in the road which was next to the pond near the trees where Bruce Moose lived, he was nowhere to be seen.

Buford turned to the others and said, "Bruce must have overslept today—just like last Saturday." The big bear began to bellow. "C'mon, slowpoke, wake up! It's time to go to the meadow to play!"

Nearby branches began moving slowly, and soon a pair of antlers emerged. A weak voice called out, "Sorry guys, I can't play today. I'm tired. And I don't feel very well."

The forest friends looked at each other, puzzled. "That doesn't sound like our Bruce Moose," said Elwood. "He used to love going down to the meadow."

"Right," exclaimed Shirl. "But this is the third Saturday in a row that Bruce has made some excuse not to play with us. Something must be wrong."

HipHop jumped in. "Maybe if I make one of my famous funny faces for Bruce, he'll forget what's bothering him and come out to play."

"Bruce," called Shirl. "You haven't come to the big meadow for the last three Saturdays. We don't think you're really sick. And you can't be that tired. What's wrong? Why don't you want to play with us?"

Finally Bruce stuck his head out of the bushes and sighed. "If I come out and play, something might happen," he said mournfully.

"Yeah," answered Norman, "we might have fun!" Norman laughed at his joke, but Bruce didn't join him.

"I meant that something bad might happen," Bruce said.

"Like what?" asked Brenda.

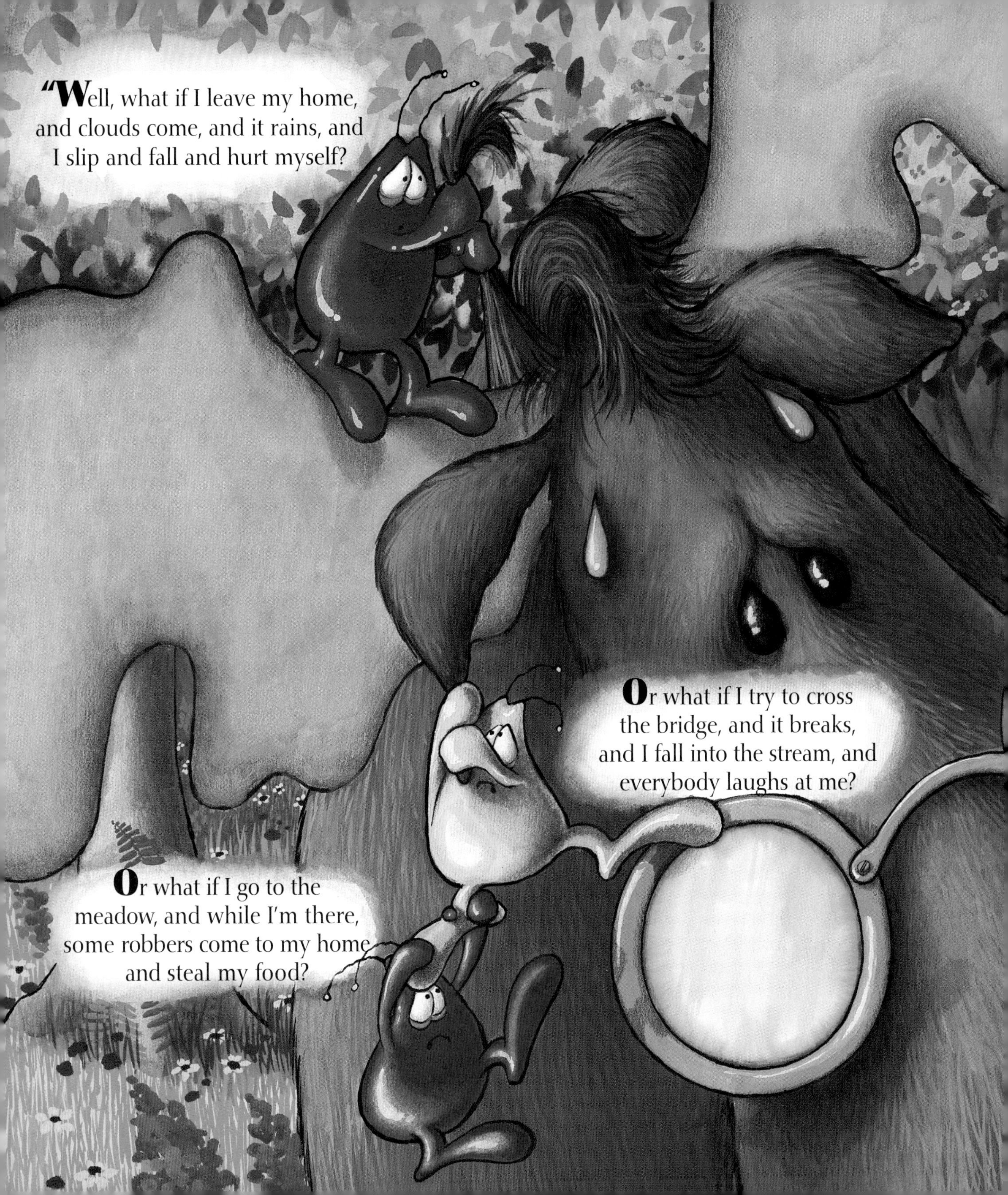

"Well, what if I leave my home, and clouds come, and it rains, and I slip and fall and hurt myself?

Or what if I try to cross the bridge, and it breaks, and I fall into the stream, and everybody laughs at me?

Or what if I go to the meadow, and while I'm there, some robbers come to my home and steal my food?

Or what if my parents run away from home while I'm gone?

Or what if I make a mistake playing a game, and you all decide you don't want to play with me?"

With each new worry he thought of, Bruce's head hung lower, as if he carried heavy weights in his antlers.

Before Bruce could name another What-If, Brenda Blue Jay blurted out, "I know what's wrong with Bruce!"

She flew to a little branch next to Bruce's worried face, looked straight into his big, brown moose eyes, and said, "You've got a serious case of the What-Ifs. You're letting those little guys boss you around and tell you what to do."

"What's a What-If?" asked Bruce.

Brenda explained, "A What-If is a tiny, imaginary creature, that makes you think of all the bad things that might happen if you do something. Sometimes it's called worry. Everybody has What-Ifs. But most of the time they stay little and harmless. If you listen to your What-Ifs, though, they get stronger and heavier."

Bruce Moose shook his head in wonder. His What-Ifs clung tightly to his antlers.

"If you listen to the What-Ifs long enough, you'll be too scared to do anything at all. They'll make your head hurt, upset your stomach, ruin your sleep, and take away your energy. You'll just stay at home and worry about all the terrible, awful, horrible things that might happen," said Brenda.

"I had that problem once," said Norman. "In those days, my nickname was Worry Worm. I worried that it might rain hard and flood my wormhole. I worried that I'd be out for a midnight crawl and a bigger animal would squish me. I worried that I'd fall into the stream right when a hungry fish came swimming by."

"What did you do?" Bruce asked.

"I didn't come out of my hole for a week. I worried about everything. I felt lower than slug slime." Then Norman stood up as straight and tall as a nightcrawler can stand and said, "Finally, I made up my mind I would not let those What-Ifs boss me around. So I told them to get lost."

"I didn't know you could do that," Bruce replied. "I thought those What-Ifs were right."

"Of course they're not right, you goofy moose," said Shirl matter-of-factly. "What-Ifs don't like the truth. They are cowards. If you tell them the truth, talk to your friends, and go ahead with your plans, the What-Ifs will go away."

"Yeah," said Norman. "They don't know what's going to happen. They just want to keep you stuck in your hole and stop you from having fun."

Elwood hadn't said anything for a while. Finally, in his mellow elk voice, he asked, "Bruce, has hiding in the woods made you feel better? Are you happier? Have the What-Ifs gone away? Or are there more of them?"

Bruce thought and thought and thought. His friends were right. Hiding hadn't helped. It had only made him feel worse.

After a long pause, Shirl said kindly, "We can't fix this problem for you, Bruce. So we're going to the meadow. Just remember that we're your friends. And we really want to see you there later. You know you can do it."

Slowly, the animal friends headed down the path, leaving Bruce alone with his What–Ifs. His head felt heavy with all the thoughts he needed to think. And the What–Ifs seemed to weigh a ton.

He glanced up and saw a What–If staring him in the eyes. Why not follow his friends' advice? he wondered.

"Listen you," Bruce said sternly. "Go away."

The What–If held on more tightly to Bruce's antler and made a nasty-looking face.

Bruce tried to remember what Shirl had said. Yell at the What–Ifs? No. Beat them off with a stick? No. Tell them the truth? Was that it? Yes!

"**H**ey! The truth is I'm going to leave my home and it won't rain. It's a beautiful, sunny Saturday," said Bruce, sounding more sure than he felt. Suddenly, with a *pop*, the What–If disappeared.

"And you up there," said Bruce, carefully walking down the path, "no one will come to my place and rob me while I'm gone."

He heard another pop and his head felt a bit lighter. "And my parents would *never* leave me alone. And my friends *will* play with me at the meadow."

Pop!

Pop!

It's working, thought Bruce

When he got to the bridge by the meadow stream, Bruce had only one What-If left. It didn't want to let him go. He thought he could hear it whispering in his ear, "You'll never get across that bridge; it's going to break. Give up. Go home."

But instead of listening, Bruce said in his deepest moose voice, "You're just plain wrong. I cross that bridge all the time, and I will again today." As the last What-If disappeared, Bruce lifted his head proudly and marched over the bridge and into the meadow where his friends were waiting for him.

All day he stayed and played tag, hide-and-go-seek, and his very favorite game, Duck Duck Moose.

Though the What-Ifs tried to bother Bruce a few more times, he only had to tell them the truth to make them disappear.

And that Saturday and all the Saturdays to follow were once again Bruce's favorite day of all in Wonder Woods.

GROWING ON:
HOW GROWNUPS CAN HELP A CHILD COPE WITH WORRY

Ask your child to give you his or her definition of worry. Ask: *Do you think worry is good or bad? Where did you learn that?*

Explain that worry is a God-given emotion which everyone experiences. There are different ways to express the worry that all of us experience. Some ways are helpful and some do harm.

Talk about these questions:

★ Read with your child the key verse for this book: "Anxiety in a person's heart weighs him down" (Proverbs 12:25, AMP).

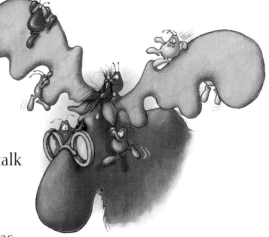

☾ Here are other Bible passages to read together and talk about: Matthew 6:25–34, Psalm 37:1–8, Proverbs 14:30; 15:15; 17:22, Philippians 4:6

★ What were some of the first signs that something was wrong with Bruce? What did his friends notice that was different about Bruce?

☾ What were some of Bruce's What-Ifs and how were they affecting him?

★ Do you ever have any What-Ifs? What are they?

☾ How did Bruce feel after he let his What-Ifs control him?

★ Discuss your child's definition of worry. You can talk about the fact that God has given us the ability to care about people and things. Perhaps your child is concerned about a pet or loved one. This is good. But when we focus on all of the

terrible, awful, horrible things (What–Ifs) that might happen, our healthy caring can turn into worry. When worry controls us, it can have a bad effect on us and on those we love. It's important to communicate that God gave us the ability to care and be concerned for others, and at times we *will* worry. It becomes a problem when we allow the worry to "take over" and control how we think and what we do.

☾ Ask: Does your mom or dad ever worry? What do they do when they worry?

★ Ask: What can happen to you if you listen to the What–Ifs too long?

*Grownups will find more information on this subject on pages 123–144 of *Raising Emotionally Healthy Kids* by H. Norman Wright and Gary J. Oliver, published by Victor Books.

Discover all the Wonder Woods books!
Ric and Rac's Woodland Adventure (Fear)
HipHop and His Famous Face (Anger)
Buford Bear's Bad News Blues (Sadness)
Bruce Moose and the What-Ifs (Worry)

Editor: Liz Duckworth
Designer: Andrea Boven
Production: Myrna Hasse

ISBN: 1-56476-462-1

1 2 3 4 5 6 7 8 9 10 Printing/Year 00 99 98 97 96